chico

Patricia Almada
Illustrated by Monique Passicot

Rigby

Chico is Omar's dog.
Chico is white.

Chico can jump.

Chico can sit.

Chico can shake.

Chico can chew
on a bone.

Chico can dig.

Chico can play
with a ball.

Chico can run
after the ball.

"Chico, Chico, come
here!" said Omar.

"Dad, where is Chico?"
said Omar.

"Mom, where is Chico?"
said Omar.

"Look here," said Mom.

"Chico is not here,"
said Omar.

"Look here," said Dad.

"Chico is not here,"
said Omar.

"Chico is here!"
said Omar.
"Chico, come out!
Come out, Chico!"